First published in France in 2004 by l'école des loisirs under the title
Je mangerais bien un enfant, © 2004 l'école des loisirs

This UK edition first published in 2008

Translation copyright © Hodder Children's Books 2008

Hodder Children's Books
338 Euston Road, London, NW1 3BH

Hodder Children's Books Australia
Level 17/207 Kent Street, Sydney, NSW 2000

A catalogue record of this book is available from the British Library.

ISBN: 978 0 340 97049 2
10 9 8 7 6

Printed in China

Hodder Children's Books is a division of Hachette Children's Books
An Hachette UK Company
www.hachette.co.uk

I Really Want to Eat a Child

For Suzanne, Zacharie and Gabriel

I Really Want to Eat a Child

by Sylviane Donnio
Illustrations by Dorothée de Monfreid

Hodder
Children's
Books

A division of Hachette Children's Books

Every morning, Mum Crocodile brought Achilles some delicious
bananas for breakfast and every morning she looked at him with pride.
'You are growing so big and strong, my son,' she said.
'And what beautiful teeth you have.'

'I know,' agreed Achilles.

But one morning, Achilles wouldn't eat a thing.
Poor Mum Crocodile was very worried.
This had never happened before!
'Are you sure you don't want a delicious banana?' she asked.
'No thanks, Mum,' replied Achilles.

'Today **I really want to eat a child!**'

'What an idea, Achilles!' she cried in surprise.
'Children don't grow on banana trees, only bananas!'

'Yes, I know,' said Achilles. 'But still, **I really want to eat a child!**'

Dad Crocodile decided to try and help. He ran to the village and brought back a sausage as big as a lorry. 'No thank you, Dad,' said Achilles shaking his head.

'Today **I really want to eat a child!**'

'But Achilles,' said his father.
'There's no such thing as a sausage made from children.'

'I don't care,' snapped Achilles. **'I really want to eat a child!'**

Luckily Dad and Mum Crocodile were clever and they came up with
a cunning plan. 'Our Achilles is a greedy little croc,' they said to each other.

'Let's make him a big scrumptious chocolate cake and
he'll completely forget this ridiculous idea!'

The cake was magnificent.
'Wow!' Achilles shouted when he saw it.
He reached out for one big delicious slice...

Then he got cross. 'Today,' he shouted,
'I really want to eat a child!'

Dad and Mum Crocodile were at the end of their tether.
'Oh! Oh!' they cried and hugged each other.
'We don't know what to do. Our dear son Achilles won't eat!'

Achilles was beginning to feel rather strange and a little bit weak.
Well, that's what happens when you don't eat your food.
'A nice swim would do me good,' he thought. And he went down to the river.

On the riverbank, he found a little girl playing all alone.
'Great!' thought Achilles. 'At last, I'm really going to eat a child!'
He hid himself in the grass and bared his teeth like a fierce beast ready to pounce.

'Oh! Just look at that,' cried the little girl, catching sight of him.
'A tiny baby crocodile! He's so sweet! And so small! I bet he doesn't eat much!'

Quick as a flash, she caught him by the tail and tickled his tummy.
'Coochie, coochie coo!' she gurgled.

Then, when she'd had enough, she threw him into the river.

'Bother!' thought Achilles. 'It wasn't meant to happen like that!'
He climbed out of the river, dripping wet and very hungry and ran back home.
'Dad! Mum! Quick,' he shouted. 'Give me some bananas! I have to grow big...

...BIG ENOUGH TO EAT A CHILD!'